I0616976

CLOUD COVER

by

Cee McAdams

WingSpan Press

Cover design by Donald Crank
8-pound spider illustration by Ayanna Freeman
Game Over illustration by Matias Perez Jr.

Published in the United States
by WingSpan Press, Livermore, CA

The WingSpan name, logo and colophon are the trademarks of WingSpan Publishing.
www.wingspanpress.com

ISBN 978-1-59594-639-3 (pbk.)
ISBN 978-1-59594-954-7 (ebk.)

First edition 2019

Printed in the United States of America

1 2 3 4 5 6 7 8 9 10

"When you reach the end of your rope, tie a knot in it and hang on."

—Franklin D. Roosevelt

YOU NEVER KNOW HOW STRONG YOU
ARE UNTIL BEING STRONG IS THE ONLY
CHOICE YOU HAVE.

—The Fresh Quotes

TABLE OF CONTENTS

Introduction: The Sticky Fingers
  Dilemma...1

Chapter One: Room Sixteen Fourteen..6

Chapter Two: The 8 Pound Spider 20

Chapter Three: A Better Mouse Trap...34

Chapter Four: Game Over 40

Chapter Five: The Boys' New Digs......55

Excerpt from the Qtr Moon Mystery
  Series 67

The Easter Bunny (Intro).....................68

The Easter Bunny.................................69

Musings from a Wounded Spirit...........78

And so I write... 80

About the Author.................................86

CLOUD COVER

(The Sticky Fingers Dilemma)

I'm not sure why I was picked for this assignment...maybe because I was the most likely person to have this kind of duty. It had to be explained to me several times before I agreed to consider it, then several more times plus a promise of a bonus before I agreed to take it and even then, my reticence was growing exponentially.' Run away' it was saying...I should have listened.

Cloud Cover

It seems that someone was caught doing something naughty; at least in the eyes of those who caught him, it was a very nasty, totally forbidden no-no... he was caught with his fingers wrapped around some ill-gotten gain along with some records. He had thoughts of far away places and beautiful people to help him enjoy his new-found wealth. He believed that he could just take it and leave town. Well apparently not! Now he is on the run, but instead of running for Argentina, he ran to friends on the local newspaper. They want to keep him alive and talking, filling volumes with details, hoping that his bosses would be rounded up, sooner rather than later, and brought in to answer a few questions. These guys were thinking PULITZER! There was only

one little problem: those bosses were not interested in talking, and certainly not interested
in seeing their faces plastered
on the front pages of the evening addition. They wanted this
guy found, silenced, and those
records recovered...they didn't
really care about the money he
stole (or so they wanted him
to believe) but wouldn't mind if
they could get it back.

It seems that these are very
determined people: determined
not to be identified, determined
not to be found and determined
to save those multi-million
dollar off-shore accounts...most
of all, determined not to allow
this small annoyance to cause
them to lose any sleep. They
knew how to take care of little
annoyances like this.

Cloud Cover

The guy had done nothing really criminal - just a little theft of a few hundred thousand, money that was not supposed to be there anyway...he saw an opportunity to help himself out of a financial bind...too many poker loses, too many wrong decisions, too much credit card debt, one too many lady-loves with too many high-dollar demands. 'What could be easier? It's just sitting there in the safe...I've got to put these files in there anyway..Just take a few thousand...who would miss it? May as well take this ledger along...I may need it for a little late reading on some cold and lonely night (as insurance no doubt) who would care? By the time anyone finds out it's miss-ing, I will be long gone' - or so he had hoped. But life has a way of playing dirty tricks on you when you least expect it. How could he know that the office manager would come back for something and catch him with his hands full of lovely, green, illegal money! Their unreported lovely green money...The Infernal Revenue Scoundrels would frown on such things!

Of course, everyone knows that there is no such thing as a hired assassin, certainly not running around in the city...pure 1930's poppycock! But just in case, these newspaper guys came up with what they hoped was an ingenious plan to keep their friend alive and win their Pulitzer...and I was supposed to be the integral part of that plan. I can hardly contain my great joy!!

CHAPTER ONE
Room Sixteen Fourteen

As soon as I heard about this bizarre incident, I had this queasy feeling that I would some- how get entangled in it. I've been in this business, in one capacity or another for 22 years, taking care of people who cannot seem to take care of themselves or manage to keep their lives on the straight and narrow. For the most part, I have really enjoyed the work... only a few moments of regret... more like 'why did I choose this job' kind of thoughts, when I've had an unusually difficult client or an exceptionally long day. This is the kind of work you have to love or you will not be effective... you will go home and know that someone has been disappointed, or worse...more often than not, it will be you. Every now and then, someone is left wondering 'how did I get myself into this and will I survive? I didn't have the answer to these questions but I knew that this was going to be one of those days and one of those clients.

I was called in by someone who never talked to me; in fact, he seemed to go out of his way to avoid me. Today he actually called me by name, invited me into his office and offered me a seat and a cup of coffee. I took a seat but refused the coffee. Right away, my left eye started to twitch...this was a very bad omen.

He wanted me to know that something had come up that he thought was perfectly suited to my skill set and my personality. He gave me the rundown, words dripping with sarcasm, on a guy whom he said could hardly wait to meet me. I felt as if I suddenly needed very tall boots because a storm of roiling malarkey was filling this room up fast. I wanted to lift my feet but instead I just sat there and nodded a lot, anxious to get this little chat over with.

☾

When I was introduced to this person, I thought he looked familiar but it was one of those inklings that slid across some ancient bridge of my memory...I didn't give it too much thought.

Cloud Cover

Sometime during the visit, it came rushing back to me. I could hardly believe it! I recognized him even though I'm sure he thought his disguise was uncrackable! He did look different...a lot of facial hair...! remembered him as being clean shaven, but he had those same warm brown eyes and friendly expression.

He looked older but he was the same guy I knew from way back when. I'm not sure if he recognized me...if he did he gave no indication. I had met him at a party of a friend of a friend. We shared some chitchat over a drink but that was so long ago.

Somewhere along the way, since we had last seen each other, life had played a really nasty joke on him...I couldn't help but feel that maybe he has totally missed the punch line. I guess worrying about staying alive after you've stolen a quarter of a million dollars from some very nasty people can not only age a man ten years but it can surely give him an inaccurate assessment of himself.

I told him who I was and a bit about why I was there but didn't try to paint pictures for him... he may have figured it out but didn't let on. I told him that from this moment on, he and I were going to be spending a lot of time together and that he was to do whatever I said needed to be done - no questions asked. I talked - he nodded a lot.

☾

Cloud Cover

On my way to his location on this cold, dark and wet morning, I had nothing on my mind except my not so new client. I had been back to see him just to get him (and me) used to the idea of this new routine. As I pulled into the parking lot, I saw a guy at a door on the other side of the building. He may have come out of that door or he may have been just hanging around. He looked up, took notice of a car pulling in, and then he started toward the parking lot, not rushing exactly – he seemed to be lurking, taking furtive glances over his shoulder, looking around as if he was trying to get his bearings, not sure he was in the right place.

He stuffed both hands in his pockets, a gesture of a nervous someone or someone acting nervous to cover his movements. Whatever the case, he looked suspicious, as he rounded the corner and headed more or less in my direction. Without really trying to make him the object of my attention, I found myself glancing in his direction.

I got a good look at him but I hoped that the tint on my windshield had obscured my face so that he did not get a good look at me. This did not feel right or more to the point, he looked really out of place and gave me a case of the willies.

❨

My new client was being housed in a facility carefully picked by his newspaper buddies. It had been mentioned to me that no one would think to look for anybody in a place like this unless he, she or they were very old, sick or just very decrepit...my client was none of these, just terrified that he was not going to be alive long enough to make his getaway to South America. His friends had promised him anonymity, protection and whatever help he needed as long as they were given the right to the story. (That Pulitzer was practically theirs!)

I busied myself with looking in my bag and getting one thing or another situated so that I would be organized when I went inside to get my day started. As it turned out, my new friend was parked only one vehicle over and one behind me so that if I slightly turned my head, I could

see him out of the side view mir-
ror. I noticed that he was in no
hurry to leave and I was getting
an uneasy feeling just sitting
there. A little voice was saying
things like 'run' and 'just drive
away' but I sat there a moment
longer while I smoothed down
those pesky little hairs on the
back of my neck.

Finally I picked up my bag and
as if on a last minute whim, I
reached into the backseat to
retrieve my jacket; I glanced
in his direction and noticed
that he was looking directly at
me. Suddenly my pulse kicked
into high gear and my feet felt
leaden but I could not just sit...I
had to either get out or start
the car and drive away. Leaving
didn't seem like the best option
anyway since he would probably

follow me if he was really up to no good, plus I would be late for work. 'Don't invite trouble' I admonished myself...'he might be waiting for a friend', although I didn't believe it for a second.

I stepped out of my car, hit the farb to lock the doors, and walked directly to the front door. I had no sooner entered when I looked back over my shoulder and I saw him get out of his vehicle and head toward the building, in no hurry, but not dawdling either.

My client's room was 1614, on the east side of the building, near the far end of the hall, the second door from an emergency entrance, so I did not have to go through the entire building to get to his room, just travel a short distance down a long corridor past the nurses' station and around the corner. No sooner had I entered the corridor, I noticed an unusual amount of goings-on, nurses running around and someone yelling 'find the doctor...we need to call the doctor!'

I rushed past all of this activity and into my client's room only to find him sitting with his back to the door, nervous, starring wild-eyed and nearly manic. My mind did not immediately connect any dots...I was not thinking that this had anything to do with him directly, but more like I had walked in on a disorganized fire drill...all I cared about at that moment was that my client looked as if he had seen Beelzebub himself and knew something was terribly out of whack. I had momentarily forgotten about the guy I had seen in the parking lot.

I went over to my client and tried to get him to calm down a bit. He was trying to tell me something but he was incoherent. I gave him a little water and then put his oxygen on, even though he didn't require oxygen...it was just part of the disguise. I was trying to think of an explanation for whatever was happening. I took a peek out into the corridor just in time to hear a nurse ask if anyone had found the doctor or called the cops and that maybe they should lock the front entry doors. I thought this odd since those doors remain open during the day. (They lock automatically when someone exits after business hours but it was not even mid-morning.) This seemed like a definite cause for alarm. Not 30 seconds later, we heard glass break.

CHAPTER TWO
The 8 Pound Spider

I grabbed my bag and my client who was sitting in a wheelchair, an addition to his disguise, and headed down the corridor toward a linen storage closet at a trot. I thought it best to get him out of the line of fire whether there was fire or not. We rushed in and I pushed aside a cart of some description, shoved the door shut and put the cart back across the door. I filled it will more blankets and whatever I could find to make it heavier, then we moved as far into the darkness as we could go and sat in complete silence. My client seemed to be only slightly

⚫

calmer; me, however, the utterly cool, supremely skilled professional, was so frantic that I could hardly keep my knees from buckling, and there was no rhyme or reason that I could see. If I cared to listen, I could hear my knees playing a staccato as I tried to remember to breathe normally and remain upright...I could not imagine what was causing all of this madness...I failed to take any particular notice of an old man in a wheel chair rolling slowly down the corridor, headed toward my client's room as we were headed in the opposite direction.

⚫

We stayed in the linen closet for what I guessed to be about 40 minutes. I could hear nothing of the noise and confusion going on out in the corridor so I decided to chance a peek. I pulled on the cart to move it aside but it would not move. I yanked a bit harder but nothing doing. Trying not to upset my client any further, not to mention trying not to arouse that 8-pound spider, I tried to push and then pull on the cart but it would not budge.

I could feel my nerves unraveling. That 8-pound spider had taken a hefty dose of steroids and had made me his captive audience. I couldn't call someone out in the corridor and announce our hiding place. This *bleeping* cart had wheels and there seemed no logical reason why it would not roll. I looked around at my client who was staring at me, panic in his eyes, expecting me to get this figured out so that we could get out of here.

I walked around to the side of the cart and noticed that one side of it had caught on the door handle; normally this would have been a good thing should someone had been trying to get in, but not so good for us...we wanted to get out...I had to find out what was happening just beyond this door.

I slowly moved the cart this way and that until it unhooked itself from the door handle, then slipped out into the corridor. I could see the bubble-gum-machine lights on squad cars through the windows at the far end of the corridor...I had no clue why the cops had been called. It was a cloudy overcast day when I arrived for work but now it just looked dark and dreary, like the sun had simply abandoned the sky overhead and moved on to other parts of the universe...it was nearly pitch black out...we must have been hiding in that closet longer than I had believed.

I saw a maintenance person in the corridor on his way to put away his cart...he told me that he had been sent to sweep up the broken glass and to clean up the blood streaks underneath the window. I asked him if he knew where the blood had come from and what all of the screaming and yelling was about but he was in too much of a hurry to stop and chat. He babbled something about a man in room 1614 but it made no sense to me. My client's room was 1614 but he was right beside me. While we were huddling in the linen closet, someone else must have been put in that room while his own room was being cleaned and his bed re-made. I suspected there was so much more to this story and that I was going to learn more than I had bargained for before too long.

Initially, my client was supposed to have been assigned to a different room but this one was the only one available when he arrived.

Apparently, the decision had been made to move him near the nurses' station so that they could keep a closer eye on him, believing that he was an actual heart patient. The nurses did not seem to know that this was a ruse which worked all the better for my client. His 'created' medical records were totally believable.

IF there had been another person in room 1614, he was apparently no longer with us but I have been unable to determine the identity of this man...he had either vanished without a trace or he was the one who needed the doctor. No one is talking...it is all very hush-hush.

The nurses stop talking about it whenever I show up. They didn't seem to be clued in to the fact that my client was not who he was supposed to be or that he was the likely reason for all of this chaos.

My client may have seen someone or knew something that he was not supposed to know... there was certainly more to his story or he just had a knack for turning green and babbling. Hopefully, he will be able to tell me later...right now he is a bundle of jangled nerves. I can't tell if we're supposed to raise the bridge or lower the river...I know with absolute certainty that this is no longer a safe place, far from it. That 8-pound spider Is on his job, not simply lurking nearby but is baring his fangs and has his evil eyes on me. I know also that I have to get to the bottom of this new development, whether or not it is a part of the same crazy mystery.

The guy I had seen in the

parking may have been the one who broke the window and bled all over the nice clean floor, which means he no doubt needed stitching up. Did the cops take him away or is he still in the building? With startling clarity, I realized that he knew I had seen him... it seemed that I had placed myself on his to-do list.

I have learned that this 8-pound spider is a formidable opponent. Once he sinks his fangs into his victim, he does not let go easily. No amount of reasoning, crying or quaking convinces him to let go. I couldn't seem to shake him off or the feeling that that was a day I should have stayed home in bed. It was too late by then...my client was in a lot of trouble and definitely needed me. Something had certainly gone horribly wrong with this fool-proof plan.

I couldn't spend a lot of time trying to figure out what to do...I just had to get the old melon working. I couldn't run up and down the corridor asking questions and risk running into someone whom I shouldn't...the only advantage I had was that I could identify the guy from the parking lot...maybe he didn't get a good look at me...

I wondered if he had been on this corridor earlier and if my client had seen him. It never occurred to me that I had been worrying about the wrong guy.

☾

Sometime around early evening,

the normal dinner time, the charge nurse came to tell me to have my client eat in his room and make sure that I stayed with him. I thought this was quite a bizarre request but I did not argue with her...after all, I was supposed to be family...my uncle/client was my first concern for reasons I believed she was totally unaware. Although I wanted more than anything to ask what all this ruckus was about, I said nothing.

Several hours had passed since we had heard the sound of breaking glass and the corridor was mostly back to normal. No cops cars were parked outside, no screaming nurses and no mention of the apparently missing or dead guy...he may not have even been sick but he was most certainly missing...I have heard nothing of who he was or even a hint of whether or not he was still alive.

CHAPTER THREE
A Better Mouse Trap

In the minds of those who devised this scheme, I'm sure it sounded clever if not foolproof... who would look for a protected person in an 'old folks home?' or so these places used to be called...full of old people for sure but some not-so-old people who had no place else to go...lots of suffering, some abuse and neglect...always places who have people working there with agendas other than the people in their care. Only this idea was full of flaws and holes like so many pairs of worn-out jeans or slices of half-eaten Swiss cheese...it had not worked nearly as well as planned. Early on, this plan fell completely apart. The enemy was not closing in on our location...he was in the den and stirring the martinis.

These guys who were looking for my client had not gone from door to door or from hospital to hotel...locating him may have been a fluke but I didn't believe it for a minute. I think they had help, the sort of help where someone knows a guy who knows a guy who can get this job done...locating him so quickly may have been a co-incidence but I wasn't buying that either. They had fewer than 2 weeks to plan this party, but the decorations were barely hung before all of the excitement began. My client was a sitting

⟨

duck and shaking like a leaf on a windy day. We were pretty much on borrowed time. I was going to have to sharpen my wits if I was going to keep him... and me, alive.

First, I needed to change his disguise ever so slightly but not enough to send up a red flag to the nurses. He continued to wear his oxygen...the nurses continued to bring his medication; he is after all, a cardiac patient. Whenever they would come in, I would just tell them that he was a bit grumpy at that moment and that I would have to 'baby him' a bit in order to get him to take his medication... as soon as he or she left, I put the pills in the commode.

He was still in a wheel chair but

he was going to have to go to therapy to become stronger so that one day he would be able to walk with the aid of a mobility device. I was getting him used to the idea that he was going to make a miraculous recovery and that we were going to escape this loony bin, with or without the blessings of his friends at the newspaper; that is, if he wanted to keep breathing.

When I started this assignment, I thought that I would be able to go home at night; on this day, I realized that I will have to take things one moment at a time...call in re-enforcements and send out for provisions as necessary, so that I can keep an eye on my uncle/client 24-7. I did, however, decide one day, that while he was having his bath, I needed to slip out to get some necessities...I had to be prepared for worse-case scenario...such is the nature of the beast that is this business.

CHAPTER FOUR

Game Over

I didn't have all of the escape details wrapped and tied in a bow but with each passing moment, they became a bit more cohesive. My uncle/client was walking with the aid of a crooked stick and sometimes a walker. He only had a few days to get in and out of therapy and used to being without that wheel chair so that when the time came, he could gather his nerves, turn off the doubts and turn on the jets, if needed.

One day, while I was sitting with my uncle/client in the therapy room, a guy came into the building; he was about 6 feet tall, thin, with wiry black hair, wearing a plaid shirt and an expression like something he had eaten left an awful aftertaste.

The admin offices in this place are near the front but around the corner from the entrance. I looked up from my magazine just in time to see him go into the office of the head guy and have a seat. He crossed his legs and made himself comfortable, as if the had done this many times. I was sitting at a place in the room at a severe angle so that he would have had to walk closer to the door in order to see me but then he was not looking for me...he was visiting an old friend.

Something started to itch at the back of my mind, a bit of a tingle, trying to pry loose a recent memory. It was there...I could almost take a hold of the thread but it was eluding me, just barely, but eluding me just the same. I tried to concentrate on my magazine but I only ended up reading the same sentence 5 times without capturing a single word. Then I heard laughter coming from the office where that guy had entered; it startled me slightly so I stood up, stretched my arms to obscure my face and sneaked a look into the office. This was the same guy I had seen in the parking lot when I first started on this assignment. He was passing a packet of some sort to the head guy. If I were a suspicious sort, I would say that this looked like a payoff.

☾

I had had several heart to heart chats with my client and had severely browbeaten the identity of the person out of him that he had seen on that day we had to high-tail it to the liner:i closet. It was someone he recognized but was afraid to tell me then or even admit to himself who he had seen. Since that day, I had also learned that his location had either been leaked or was not a secret from the beginning and that his safety had been compromised almost from the very first day.

Cloud Cover

When he was done explaining, I realized that something was missing from his story. I had passed this person on the corridor on that day and I had seem him on other days with no clue that he was the one we were supposed to be hiding from or that he had been paid to eliminate the problem that was my uncle/client It is tragic that someone else got in the way either a case of incompetence or a case of mistaken identity. A much larger tragedy was that no one seemed worried...I could not imagine why or why not... there should have been raised eyebrows at the very least or more likely, outrage.

I had over-heard a couple of the nurses talking one day about the old guy who had disappeared and learned that he had been the old man in my uncle/client's room, who had more than likely been mistaken for him. I felt terrible for not having noticed him in the corridor on that day but I was so frantic at that moment that I all I could think of was getting my uncle/client to safety.

((

According to the way my uncle/client had explained it to me, this entire scenario had been worked out to minute detail by his friends; to me it was not to be believed. What would newspaper guys know about situations like this! They made too many mistakes. Their plan left too many questions unasked and no answers for any of them.

Cloud Cover

The supposed assassin was none other than an employee of this facility and apparently an associate of the people from which my uncle/client had borrowed a quarter of a million. I knew I would have to double my resolve to get him out of this place and to somewhere safer... maybe nowhere was entirely safe. We were running out of time...the numbers were falling fast...but they were playing it as if this was a done deal. Maybe it was but I would not make it easy for them.

I had moved my uncle/client around a lot over the days he had been in this place and tried to keep him in a large group of people almost constantly. Whenever I had to visit the ladies' room, I would take him to

((

the nurses' station and tell one of the nurses that he was having a little discomfort or some other fabricated issue. He or she would take the time to check him out but I knew this would not take too long so I had to always hurry and finish the business at hand and get back to him post haste.

((

On this day, the plans were finalized. I had everything packed and ready to go. I had to call in some assistance because getting him to check himself out might be tricky. I had trimmed his beard, moved his wheel chair aside, put a hat on his head and handed him his walking stick with orders to use it if it became necessary. I had chosen a day when I knew the head guy would be in meetings most of the day so we would not have to try to sneak past him.

My assistant had called an ambulance and it was waiting at the front. Their doctor had examined him and noticed that my uncle/client's BP was really elevated, which was not good but made things so much easier at checkout, so all he had to do was sign whatever needed to be signed and be discharged to the hospital...no problems...things went much more smoothly than expected.

We had planned to tell a different story but thankfully we didn't need to use it...it was going to be that all of the extra stress of physical therapy had caused him to feel really tired and thought he needed to get a thorough checkup...he was worried about his heart...frankly, I think it was the extra stress of worrying about staying alive that caused his BP to spike and his heart was probably truly working harder than it should.

In any case, my assistant put him in the ambulance and his belongings in my vehicle. Then I got into the ambulance with him and my assistant drove my vehicle. So far so good.

We drove slowly out of the parking lot and tried to look casual, just on our way to the hospital which was close by. When we reached the next intersection, which was a block from our not-so-safe house, I told the driver that we would need to step on it and not to spare the horses when we hit the interstate. Of course this was not a regular ambulance but painted to resemble the real thing...upon closer inspection, an expert could probably tell but lucky for us, no experts were on hand.

I looked back so see if my assistant was behind us or if anyone had followed us out, but no one had come outside to see which way we had gone. We made the turn onto a mostly empty side street and headed in the opposite direction from the hospital.

When we made it to the interstate, the driver hit the sirens and we were running hot. We cooled off after about 25 miles, killed the sirens and turned into a business/medical complex where my assistant and more of my associates were waiting for us to arrive. Only then did I realize that I had been holding my breath.

They took my client (who by this time had resigned as my uncle) into one of the offices. He was shown to a bathroom where he shaved off his beard... he also had no further need for his walking stick but kept it anyway...it was a bit unusual... it depicted a mongoose having a mostly failed attempt at eating a cobra.

This or someplace nearby, was where he was going to stay until it was time to take the next step, court or whatever, either rat out his former employers or spend

Cloud Cover

some time in the hoosegow himself, and then maybe leave the country afterward...only time would tell.

I was not privy to those details... my time with him was finished and not a moment too soon for my taste. I bid him ado, made my exit and went home. I was finally going to get in a hot bath and get rid of this 8-pound spider.

CHAPTER 5

The Boys' New Digs

It took nearly 2 months for that little merry-go-round to come to an abrupt halt. It hit the papers and the local news with a splash. Several indictments were handed down...their mugs were plastered on the front page. Each rat had squealing on the other, trying to save himself from a long stretch behind bars, all howling that he had been framed and certainly not involved in any part of this or any other kind of criminal activity. Their guy inside did a lot of finger-pointing but it did not save him...he and his cohorts were all going to be wearing jailhouse blue for awhile and all looked rather spiffy.

☾

It seems that the old man who had been sitting in room 1614 had been identified. I never learned why he was in that room - maybe just to visit my client...maybe they had been friendly at some point. For some other inexplicable reason, the facility thought that his family would not be concerned and curious as to what had happened to him, would not come around to see him or would ask no questions whatsoever. That was by no means the case. The family has squawked and loudly. The newspaper guys made a bigger deal of this incident than originally intended and our not-so-safe-hiding place was crawling with investigators for days to come. Some of the ex employees are still looking for other jobs.

Our assassin was none other than the head guy at that facility. One of his friends/associates has ratted him out in order to save himself...it seems that he was desperate for money so it had been easy enough for them to convince him that it was a simple assignment...after all, he was already on-site and no one would ever suspect him... he was just supposed to make sure that he got his hands on the money and those records as quickly as possible without arousing suspicion. He would walk away clean and they would all be richer. Well best laid plans or not counting the chickens before they hatch or some such cornball logic seemed appropriate but I don't know which...it hardly matters to any of them or to anyone else.

Our guy had in fact located the duffle bag with some of the money in it...he had hurriedly searched the room the day that we were huddling in the linen closet and had assumed that it contained ALL of the stolen money as well as the records. I can only surmise that he felt that his search was successful after he took a quick peek inside, so he picked it up and rushed out of the room after having snuffed out the wrong guy...he did not realize that he was going to be scurrying down the corridor with a duffle bag full of, not those big bucks, but only a small portion of the stolen money, a magazine or two, plus some socks and t-shirts.

On that day with all of the commotion that he and his cohort had created, he slipped into room 1614, believing that the person in there was my client but he had guessed wrong; in fact, all of his guesses had been wrong. The records were hidden someplace else and the rest of the money was in a safe deposit box. Not only that, but I had discovered this little stash early on and had rearranged the contents of that duffle bag so that [some of] the money was on top, but mostly what he had in his possession were a couple of my clients t-shirts, socks, and a couple of magazines.

He must have surely realized his mistake only a nanosecond after the old man had stopped breathing, but by then it was too late. I do not surmise that his conscience was any kind of a burden...I do not believe that this predatory creature was born with a conscience and therefore he was and Is incapable of any remorse...creatures like him, running around disguised as human, have no morals and no clue about ethics or care in the least about human suffering... the invisible line that most of us will not cross did not and does not exist for him...all that mattered to him was an old man was standing (or sitting) between him and the money he so desperately wanted, but I can only imagine that angry dragon in his gut getting a bit perturbed when he realized that he had failed to recover the money or the records...a feeling sort of like that 8-pound spider that had crawled up my back and sank his fangs into my neck, only so much worse.

Having to confront his associates with news of his failure could not have produced a very warm and fuzzy feeling.

My client had seen him earlier and had recognized him. I suppose that as soon as he realized his mistake, he knew that he would have to rush out of that room and to the nurses' station with the old man and try to cover his tracks, so he started ordering the nurses to call the doctor...the old man had slumped in his wheel chair but he had not simply stopped breathing...he had had help.

On that day, the head guy was making his escape down the corridor just as I rounded the corner. It was no wonder my client was scared speechless. I had passed our assassin in the corridor and didn't know who he was at the time.

No one has told how he was connected to the original crooks... no one seems to want to talk about it. Apparently, that nest of thieves had planned to split almost a half million dollars in what was later described as campaign contributions they had not turned over to the proper people, but their plan had been spoiled by my client who almost lost his life over money he may never get a chance to spend.

Our head guy's accomplice had been waiting as the handoff guy, to take the duffle bag containing the money and the records, make the payoff at that time the job was finished, since they both thought the job was done, plus act as backup if needed, but he never made it back into the building if in fact he had been in there earlier. When the plan developed a hitch, he had to devise a minor distraction... breaking the window seemed as good a diversion as any at that moment...cutting himself was not in the planning...but he was long gone by the time the cops arrived.

I've decided to retire and take up gardening...I'm learning to play in the dirt and watch the flowers bloom instead of dodging assassins and baby-sitting lite-fingered clients. I'm so much happier reading about these shenanigans in the paper.

Take a sneak peek at the
excerpt from the upcoming

THE QTR MOON

MYSTERY SERIES

THE EASTER BUNNY

Intro

This is the story of a well-known character we see only once a year...and then only for a few days...the rest of the time, he has chosen to keep his life completely hidden from the prying eyes of the curiosity seekers. The story goes that he only comes around for a few days in the early spring and then fades away like old news. No one knows where he comes from or where he goes when his 'job' is done. I think it's time we unraveled this mystery a bit and get a closer look at this most unlikely icon. We may be in for quite a surprise.

THE EASTER BUNNY

A Qtr Moon Mystery

Each year, as soon as it's time to spring forward, we get our happy smiles on because we know that soon it will be time to dye the eggs, get the baskets ready, shop for the hottest outfits, and look for the most colorful candy...it's time for the Easter Bunny to make his appearance and hide the eggs. No one knows just where he lives, how he travels and most of all, how he feels about all of the nonsense he has been accused of doing. All we know is that he magically appears just in time for Easter.

So what would happen to all of those blue, green, pink and pur- ple eggs if the Easter Bunny gets caught in rock slide or carried away by a dive-bombing hawk or delayed because he had to move the family to a new home before going off to Yonderland to do the egg hiding? Is there a backup bunny or will the Mother Squirrel be called into action. I think not! Perish the thought! It would just be unthinkable.

Has anyone ever given any thought to what he does with his life the rest of the year? Has any- one ever offered to pay for his travel? Does he have any kind of a retirement plan when he is too old or too crotchety to do this job anymore? Does he even have a contract? Well I can offer only a few wild guesses, none of which follows any particular line of logical progression: he celebrates birthdays, eats lots of carrots and lettuce, walks the kids to school, dances with his spouse (who knew bunnies got married I'm sure you're asking) takes frequent naps and pretty much keeps himself in shape for those days when he is expected to work really hard lifting all of those baskets of eggs he has to hide, totally for the amusement of so many human kids. Not that he does any of these things, but people across the country ex-pect someone to do it so he has been going through the motions year after year...this time he de-cided enough is enough.

Well just before the big day, he reluctantly put his gym membership on hold, packed a toothbrush, said goodbye to the spouse and the kids and headed out to survey the areas [of wherever there is tall grass or make-believe haystacks or any other kind of structure humans have devised for him to hide the eggs.] He took a look around and then ushered forth a very loud sigh. He does not want to disappoint the human kids but cannot decide whether to sit down and cry or just run away again. His heart breaks a little each time he has to play this game with himself but he decided that this time, things were going to be different. He would not betray himself or go home devastated and feeling like a failure. He wanted to take out a billboard ad or call a news conference to tell the world about his decision but felt that that would cause too much of a stir, downright panic perhaps, so he just got in touch with me so that I could be his spokesperson. He was determined to set things right.

He stopped by for awhile and we decided to hang out in the backyard and do a bit of catching-up. I crunched on a few carrots and he had a snack of Timothy [grass], apple chips and a tall glass of carrot juice. We talked about things in general. He told me that the spouse worries when he is gone too long and that he needed to get home before dark to get the family tucked in safely.

Before he left, he asked me to pass along a few tidbits of

information to all of those who have besmirched him for so long…he also hopes that it will help to dispel the rumor that he likes chocolate, with or without marshmallows, with or without peanut butter…he definitely does not! It gives him a bellyache, a bit of the cobblywoggs, makes his hair fall out and causes cavities which leads to dental bills that he cannot afford. More than anything else, he found this bit of news most distressing and simply could not imagine how such rumors got started. Further, he wanted me to be sure to let all of you know that neither he nor his spouse lay, boil, color, or hide eggs, nor do they search for eggs, dyed or otherwise. He does not shop for baskets, make baskets or deliver baskets and has no clue where they all come from...neither he nor any member of his family has ever seen an egg or a basket.

He was quite over-wrought...I thought perhaps I would have to spike his carrot juice to get him to calm down. Reluctantly, he sipped his juice, took deep breaths and got his anger under control.

Mr. Rabbit has heard that there is an impostor going around pretending to be him...he does not know who this impostor is who dresses up to look like him and makes believe that he is hiding eggs. Apparently, the impostor is believable...perhaps he is a groundhog or a gopher who has a family that depends on him...perhaps this was the only job available or perhaps he simply enjoys the mimicry and does not give much thought to the possible danger. Whatever the reason, Mr. Rabbit has no problem allowing him to continue with the charade. He has also heard that some of the humans have set a trap to capture this impostor on film as he is hiding the eggs or pretending to do so. This made him very sad and left me totally awestruck, having to sit and watch his heart break.

I've known a rabbit or two myself and I can speak with some semblance of authority that Mr. Rabbit just wants to go home, hug the spouse and play with the kids. He wants to enjoy his munchies and get as much rest as possible because soon he will have a lot of birthdays to celebrate and a lot of presents to gift wrap. He will be so busy with the celebrations and so tired afterward that he will just likely take a nap and do lots of cuddling for long moments.

☾

Mr. Rabbit has now retired from any and all human activities, not that there were any. He no longer participates in the pretenses involving eggs or baskets and lives with his family in a beautiful area where they can all enjoy the spring grasses without thinking about having to go out and do the impossible. At last count, Mr. Rabbit had 8 little ones and they keep him hopping. I, for one, certainly wish him well.

MUSINGS
FROM
A
WOUNDED
SPIRIT

...AND SO I WRITE

Today I sit by my window, watching the shadows from the trees grow longer while reveling in the rhythm of the flute as it reverberates through my soul. It seems that no matter the effort, the day or the time, my mind clings to the image of you standing there in the isle...I get no respite, day or night. I see you everywhere I go so the 'entity' in my mind keeps trying to formulate the most appropriate scenario for actually meeting you, everything from a simple 'hello' to a seductive embrace. All I really wanted so much to do at that moment was run to you and melt in your pocket, but I feared a rebuff. My days are consumed with thoughts of you and my nights are filled with dreams of how you enhance my life. As long as you insisted on being on my mind, I needed to transfer some of those thoughts and emotions to paper. Sometimes I can easily segue from reality to my fictional world but once ensconced in my world of make-believe, the reverse sometimes requires great effort and concentration and is sometimes unsuccessful...and so I write.

Recently I read a story about a young man who was smitten

by a young lady but was too intimidated by her beauty to approach her, so rather than risk allowing her to get away, he summoned his courage and wrote a whimsical poem for her, then read it to her at a time when he felt that she would be his captive audience. After that moment, they were inseparable. Such is my desire, to totally capture you imagination...and so I write...

The day I saw you, I did not have a poem prepared - sadly I don't do poems, and you were able to escape before I made a fool of my self...but I cannot escape the world built only of my imagination...and so I write...

Hesitation is truly a cousin of fear but my fear has manifested itself in the form of sweet and sometimes erotic dreams that have no chance of coming true. I can do nothing to quell this fear that I will never see you again and my heart breaks a little . I write about you or rather about what I see in my mind's eye. If I could, I would probably send you roses with syrupy messages but then you would think I'm a stalker and a bit unhinged. I cannot send flowers...and so I write...

It is my fervent hope along with a small prayer, that I will see you again, but if it never happens, I know that we will continue to have this awesome love affair, seething with passion, but only as it exists in the vibrant world of my imagination. I know I must continue to believe or it will leave a bruise on my soul... and so I write...

Not long ago, I read a fortune cookie insert, which said: 'DON'T GIVE UP...THE BEGINNING IS ALWAYS THE HARDEST.' Food for thought indeed... my heart is already doing backward flips at the very thought of at last, the beginning! I will then be able to abruptly transition from the melancholy and away from the crate of tissue that I have stashed beside my bed...I will no longer need to wipe away tears before they escape down my cheeks. My fractured heart will mend...the longing in my heart, the ache in my soul can then morph into smiles and I will be able to blossom like a morning glory when it sees the sunrise.

I know I must write but the feel of your hand in mine or the delicious aura of the first embrace or the taste of that first kiss will linger and will surely pause this run-away train that is this story, our story...but soon I must write again.

Cee

ABOUT THE AUTHOR

Cee McAdams is an Air Force veteran. During her first year of service, she was chosen as one of the outstanding women of the Air Force and is a charter member of the Women's Memorial in Washington DC. She began writing around the age of 10, mostly as an outlet for an ever expanding imagination. She was published in a national magazine at the age of 14. She graduated from Cameron University in

Oklahoma where she received a Writing Achievement Award from the English Department. She presently resides in Dallas Texas.

www.ingramcontent.com/pod-product-compliance
Lightning Source LLC
Chambersburg PA
CBHW030538180626
46810CB00005B/1925